Ghost Pony

Do you love ponies? Be a Pony Pal!

PONY PALS

Ghost Pony

Jeanne Betancourt

illustrated by Paul Bachem

A
LITTLE APPLE
PAPERBACK

SCHOLASTIC INC.
New York Toronto London Auckland Sydney

ISBN 0-590-37462-1

Text copyright © 1997 by Jeanne Betancourt.
Illustrations copyright © 1997 by Scholastic Inc.
All rights reserved. Published by Scholastic Inc.
PONY PALS and LITTLE APPLE PAPERBACKS
are trademarks and/or registered trademarks of Scholastic Inc.

12 11 10 9 8 7 6 5 4 3 2 1   7 8 9/9 0 1 2/0

Printed in the U.S.A.

First Scholastic printing, November 1997

Thank you to Liz Shapiro of the Sharon Historical Society, William Trowbridge, and Pat Wilson for sharing their knowledge of the past.

For my Pony Pal, Meg Charlton.
She inspired me to write this story.

Contents

Ghost Pony

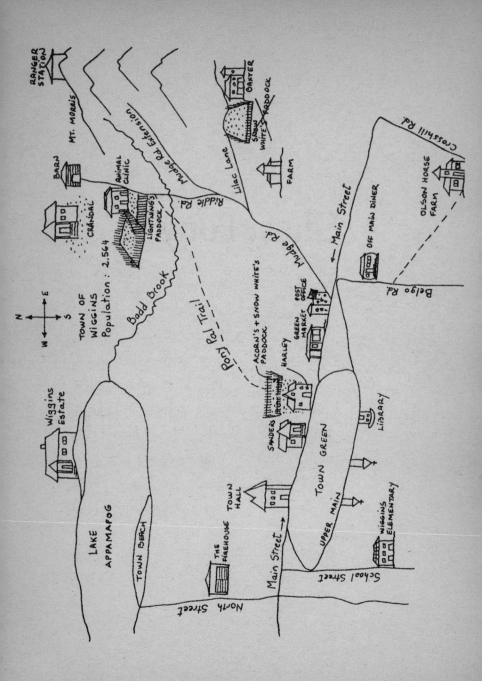

Beware!

Lulu Sanders' grandmother came out of her house onto the back porch. "So where are the Pony Pals off to today?" she asked.

Lulu and her Pony Pal, Anna Harley, were sitting on the porch steps packing their saddlebags. "We're going to ride on the trails near Mt. Morris," said Lulu. "And dig for old stuff where Morristown used to be."

"We've already found these things," said Anna. She took three old objects out of her saddlebag.

Lulu pointed to one of them. "A hand-made nail," she said.

Then, Anna held up a small wooden toy. "And this is one of those tops you spin with a string," she explained.

Lulu picked up the third object. "And this looks like part of a cup," she said.

"We dug them all up where the Ridley Farm used to be," said Anna. "That's our favorite place to dig."

"You have found some interesting things," said Grandmother Sanders.

"Did people live in Morristown when you were little?" Lulu asked.

"Morristown was deserted long before I was born," she said. "No one has lived there for over a hundred and fifty years."

"That means the things we dug up are *really* old," Anna said.

"They certainly are," said Grandmother Sanders. "You should show what you found to Janet McGee at the Wiggins Historical Society. She puts things like these in the museum."

"That's a good idea," said Lulu. "And I bet we'll find a lot more stuff to bring her."

As Anna put the objects back in her saddlebag, she looked up at Grandmother Sanders. "Did you ever go to Morristown to play when you were little?" Anna asked.

"Oh, no!" Grandmother exclaimed. "Some of my friends went there. But I was too scared. I heard too many ghost stories about Morristown."

"Ghost stories!" said Anna.

Grandmother Sanders nodded and then turned to head back into the house. "A lot of people believe that Morristown is haunted."

"I'm not afraid of ghosts," said Lulu as she buckled her saddlebag. She looked over at her pony, Snow White, who was standing next to Anna's pony, Acorn, in the paddock. It was time for a trail ride. "Let's go," Lulu told Anna. "Pam will be waiting for us."

"Maybe we shouldn't go to Morristown today," said Anna. "We should probably show Ms. McGee what we found."

Lulu smiled at Anna. "Did my grand-mother scare you?"

"Maybe a little," said Anna. "I sort of believe in ghosts."

"She was kidding around with us," Lulu told Anna. "Besides, we've been in those woods many times and we've never heard or seen anything like a ghost."

"That doesn't mean we won't," Anna whispered.

The two friends saddled up their ponies and rode onto Pony Pal Trail. The mile-and-a-half trail went from Acorn and Snow White's paddock to a big field behind Pam's house.

As they rode along the trail, Lulu looked forward to a fun day of riding with her Pony Pals. Lulu loved animals and being outdoors. She learned a lot about nature from her father. He studied and wrote about wild animals. Lulu's mother died when Lulu was four years old. After that, Lulu traveled all over the world with her father. But when Lulu turned ten, her father said she should live in one place for a while. That was when she came to Wiggins to live with her grandmother.

Lulu had been to many places with her dad. But she never saw or heard a ghost. And she didn't think she was going to see one in Morristown. She moved Snow White into a trot.

"Let's go," Anna instructed Acorn. Acorn picked up speed to keep up with Snow White. Anna was thinking about ghosts, too. When she was five she was sure she saw a ghost go out her window. She drew a picture of that ghost to show her parents. Anna loved to draw. She wished that she could draw all day instead of going to school. Anna was dyslexic, so writing and reading were extra hard for her.

While Anna and Lulu were riding to Pam's house, Pam was in the Crandals' barn saddling up her pony, Lightning. Pam liked school, but she liked riding and being around horses even better. Her mother was a riding teacher and her father was a veterinarian so Pam knew all about horses. Pam had had her own pony for as long as she could remember. Now she tightened Lightning's girth, gave her pony a loving pat on the neck, and led her out of the barn. She saw Anna and Lulu riding across the field.

Pam swung onto the saddle and galloped toward her friends. As the Pony Pals rode toward Riddle Road, Anna told Pam what Lulu's grandmother said about ghosts in Morristown.

Pam laughed. "Maybe we'll see the ghost that was in your bedroom, Anna."

"Or a bunch of new ones," teased Lulu.

"I can't help it," said Anna. "I believe in ghosts. If you saw one, you would, too."

"Don't worry, Anna," said Pam. "If we meet any ghosts we'll use our Pony Pal Power on them."

"They won't have a chance," added Lulu with a giggle.

Anna giggled too, but she was still a little afraid.

The Pony Pals soon came to the trail that led to Morristown. Pam turned Lightning onto the trail. Anna went second and Lulu followed.

Half an hour later the Pony Pals were tying their ponies to trees. They stepped over a low rock wall and stood where the Ridley farmhouse used to be. All that was left of the house were parts of the stone foundation and a crumbling stone fireplace. The girls took digging tools out of their saddlebags.

"Let's dig over near the fireplace," said Pam.

Lulu and Anna agreed.

They had only been digging for a little while when they heard a strange rustling of leaves. They stopped digging.

"What was that noise?" whispered Anna.

"Maybe it's the wind," said Pam.

"There's no wind today," said Anna.

"Maybe it was our ponies," said Lulu.

The three girls looked toward their ponies. They were standing perfectly still.

Lulu noticed that Snow White's ears were pointed forward. She was listening, too.

The leaves rustled again. Then there was a new sound. *"Oh-oo-oo. Oh-oo-oo."* It was the eeriest noise Anna had ever heard. Lulu felt a shiver go through her. Pam wondered if her imagination was playing tricks on her.

The three girls looked at each other. Someone or *something* was in the woods with them.

Spooked

"It's a ghost!" whispered Anna. She grabbed Pam's arm.

"It's not a ghost," said Pam.

"It sounded like one," said Anna.

"Did you ever hear a ghost?" Pam asked.

"No," admitted Anna. "But if I did, that's what it would sound like."

"There's no such thing as ghosts," said Pam. "An owl probably made that noise."

"*Oh-oo-oo. Oh-oo-oo.*"

Anna trembled and moved even closer to

her friends. "That doesn't sound like an owl to me," she said.

Lulu squeezed Anna's hand. "I don't think it's an owl," she said. "My dad has a tape recording of different owl calls and none of them sound like that."

"Then it's another kind of bird we've never heard before," said Pam matter-of-factly. "Or maybe it's the wind. Or an animal. But it's not a ghost."

Pam picked up her hand shovel and started to dig again. Anna and Lulu went over to the ponies to make sure they were all right. Snow White's ears were relaxed again. Acorn and Lightning were calm, too.

"I guess that was just a noise in the woods," Lulu told Anna.

"Hey, I found something!" exclaimed Pam. "Look." She held up a rusty fork.

Anna and Lulu ran over to her.

Lulu took the fork from Pam and looked at it. "Let's add it to our list," she said.

"Okay," said Anna. "I'll draw it."

"And I'll dig with you," Lulu told Pam. "Maybe we'll find some more silverware."

Anna took the notebook out of her saddlebag and sat with her back against the stone wall. She opened the notebook and looked over what they had put in it so far.

handle of cup
found four feet from fireplace,
middle of room

A toy top found near door opening.

Handmade iron nail found near fireplace.

Anna picked up her pencil and began to draw the fork. When she finished the drawing, she held the notebook up for Lulu and Pam to see.

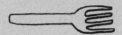

"Perfect," said Pam. She came over and sat next to Anna. "I'll write the label and where we found it," she said.

"I feel like someone is watching us," Anna whispered to Pam.

Pam stood up and looked all around. She didn't see anyone. "You're still scared because of that strange noise," she told Anna.

Lulu's hand shovel hit something solid. "I think I found something else," she said. She took out scoops of earth. "It's big. And made of metal." Lulu pulled an object out of the ground and held it up. "It's a horseshoe!" she exclaimed.

Suddenly, Acorn nickered and snorted.

Anna jumped to her feet. She ran to her pony. Pam and Lulu followed her.

A pony's whinny pierced the air. It didn't come from any of the girls' ponies and it was the weirdest whinny the Pony Pals had ever heard. Chills ran down Pam's spine. Lulu's heart skipped a beat. Anna screamed. Snow White tried to pull herself free from her tether. Acorn shook his head. And Lightning pawed the ground.

The girls and ponies heard the spooky whinny again.

"It's a ghost!" shouted Anna.

"It can't be!" exclaimed Pam.

"Let's get out of here!" said Lulu.

And without saying another word, the Pony Pals untied their ponies, mounted, and galloped out of the woods.

Ghost Town

The Pony Pals rode through the woods as quickly as they could. Their ponies were happy to go fast. They wanted to get away from Morristown, too. The girls didn't slow their ponies down until they reached Riddle Road.

"That was the scariest sound I've ever heard," said Lulu.

"It was a ghost!" said Anna. "I know it was!"

"It couldn't have been a ghost," said Pam. "Remember there's no such thing as ghosts."

The Pony Pals were all talking at once.

Pam put her hand up. "We have to stay calm."

"Let's go to the diner to talk," said Lulu.

"Good idea," said Anna. She and Acorn led the way. Anna's mother owned Off-Main Diner. The food at the diner was delicious, so the Pony Pals liked to go there to eat and talk.

When they reached the diner, the girls tied their ponies to the hitching post. Lulu and Pam went around to the back to get buckets of water for the ponies. Anna went inside to tell the cook what they wanted to eat.

When Pam and Lulu came into the diner, their sandwiches were ready. The three girls took their plates to a booth and sat down. It was time for a Pony Pal Meeting.

Lulu leaned forward. "That was the *ghost*-iest sound I've ever heard," she said.

"It was a *real* ghost!" said Anna. "For sure."

"I think it was just the wind whistling

through the trees," said Pam. "Or our imaginations."

"We couldn't all imagine the same thing," said Anna.

"Maybe it's someone trying to scare us," said Pam. "Like Tommy Rand and Mike Lacey." Tommy and Mike were mean-acting eighth-grade boys who liked to pester the Pony Pals.

"I don't think that they're smart enough to think up something like that," said Lulu.

"Besides, they're on that eighth-grade trip to Washington, D.C.," added Anna.

"If it's not Tommy and Mike," said Pam. "Who is it?"

"It's a ghost pony," said Anna. "It whinnied when Lulu dug up the horseshoe. Maybe that was the ghost pony's old horseshoe! And it doesn't want us to dig there."

"A ghost pony?" said Pam. "I don't think so."

"My grandmother said that a lot of people think there are ghosts in the Morristown woods," Lulu reminded Pam.

"Let's go back to our dig after lunch," said Pam. "I bet we don't hear that noise again. And I bet we'll find evidence that someone *was* there. Someone who wanted to scare us."

Anna shuddered. "I don't want to go back," she said.

Lulu looked at Anna and then Pam. "Maybe we should go to the Historical Society instead," she said. "We can show Ms. McGee the things we found and ask her about Morristown."

"And about ghosts," added Anna.

"Okay," said Pam. "But she'll tell you there aren't any ghosts there or anyplace else. The ghost stories are all made up."

After lunch the Pony Pals went to the Harleys' and put their ponies in the paddock. The Wiggins Historical Society was in an old house next to the library on Upper Main Street. The Pony Pals took a shortcut across the town green. The front door to the Historical Society was open so they walked right in. Ms. McGee was standing in the doorway to the front parlor. She had on an old-fashioned long dress.

"Welcome, girls," Ms. McGee said. "Everything in this house is the way it would have been in 1850. That's nearly a hundred and fifty years ago." She patted the skirt of her dress. "Even my clothes." She smiled. "And of course *I'm* not a hundred and fifty years old."

"We like old things," said Anna.

"We've been doing a dig out in Morristown," said Lulu. "On the Ridley Farm."

"And we found these," said Pam. She handed Ms. McGee five plastic bags with the nail, top, cup handle, fork, and horseshoe. Ms. McGee looked at each item carefully. "This is so interesting," she said. "There were iron ore mines on Mt. Morris, and the people who worked in the iron ore industry lived in Morristown. Ridley Farm was the biggest farm out there."

"How come everybody left?" asked Lulu.

"The iron ore business closed up," said Ms. McGee. "So the workers went where

they could find new jobs. The only people left in Morristown were the farmers. Unfortunately there weren't enough farms to keep the school and stores going. Besides, it was pretty hilly and rocky in there for farming. Folks sold off their land and moved to town. So Morristown became a ghost town."

"A ghost town!" exclaimed Anna.

Ms. McGee laughed. "Not real ghosts, dear," she said. "Sometimes when a town is deserted, we call it a *ghost town*."

"My grandmother said there are a lot of ghost stories about Morristown," said Lulu.

"I suppose there are," said Ms. McGee. "But I don't believe them. You shouldn't either."

The Pony Pals exchanged a glance. They decided not to tell Ms. McGee about the eerie sounds they had heard.

"Would you like to know more about Morristown?" asked Ms. McGee. "I have some material on the town."

"That would be great," said Lulu.

The girls followed Ms. McGee to her office. She gave each girl a pair of white cotton gloves. "Some of the things we have here are very fragile," she explained. "So we wear gloves when we touch them." While the Pony Pals put on the gloves, Ms. McGee opened a glass case and took out a leather photo album. She handed it to Pam. "Why don't you start with this," she said.

The Pony Pals sat on the couch. Pam opened the photo album. In one picture, a horse-drawn carriage stood in front of a general store. Underneath the picture it read: "General Store. Morristown. 1850." In another picture a man walked behind a plow pulled by a horse.

While the Pony Pals looked at the album, Ms. McGee was going through her file drawer. "We have a file on Ridley Farm," she said.

"I hope you can find it quickly," said Anna. "We're especially interested in stories about ponies on Ridley Farm."

Ms. McGee pulled out a file and flipped through it. "I think there was something in this file about a pony," she said.

"We'd be very interested in that," said Lulu.

"Here it is!" exclaimed Ms. McGee. "Yes. And the pony's name was Angel. That's what I remembered." Ms. McGee handed Pam a photocopy of a newspaper article. "I have more visitors. You girls read this and I'll be back."

Lulu and Anna moved closer to Pam. The Pony Pals couldn't wait to find out about the pony named Angel.

An Angel Watches Over Her

Miss Lillian Parsons of Morristown was stranded in her mountain home during last week's big snowstorm. Folks thereabouts were worried for their elderly neighbor. So on Sunday afternoon, ten-year-old Emily Ridley drove her sleigh up to Miss Parsons' place. The sleigh, which carried food for Miss Parsons, was drawn by Emily's pony, Angel.

Angel was a nine-year-old Morgan pony. Mr. and Mrs. Ridley had given Emily the pony for Christmas. Emily and Angel were a familiar sight in Morristown. The young girl often rode her pony to the schoolhouse. "Once when I didn't ride her, she unhitched the gate and followed me to school," Emily said.

Angel also pulled the plow in Ridley fields. "That pony could do the work of a big horse," said Mr. Ridley. "She was as strong as she was sweet."

"And she knew her way around the hills," said Mrs. Ridley.

"We trusted Angel," said Mr. Ridley. "That's why we let Emily drive her up to Miss Parsons."

"And Miss Parsons was so fond of Emily," added Mrs. Ridley. "We knew they would have a good visit."

The trip up the mountain went smoothly for pony and driver. Miss Parsons was most grateful for the provisions. "It was such a lovely visit," said Miss Parsons. "That Ridley girl is so kind. I am so sorry that her troubles came because of helping me."

Emily's troubles started on the return trip. At the bend in the trail, Angel slipped on a patch of ice.

"That's when the sleigh tipped," said Emily. "It was the last thing I remember."

The young girl hit her head on a tree and lost consciousness. Perhaps Angel tried to wake Emily with nudges and hot breath. We'll never know.

Angel was also injured in the accident. Nevertheless, that brave pony made her way down the mountain, dragging the turned-over sleigh behind her. Angel made it all the way back to Ridley Farm. No one was in the barn, so she went to the house. Angel neighed and whinnied until someone took notice of her.

"She all but knocked on the front door," said Mr. Ridley. "I believe she would have done that next if we hadn't heard her neighing."

"The minute we saw Angel we knew that Emily was in trouble," said Mrs. Ridley.

"But Emily had our only sleigh," added Mr. Ridley. "And now it was broken. So our other daughter, Meg, and the Missus ran to the Warners to ask for their help. I took off Angel's harness. I was so distracted with worry for my girl that I didn't notice that Angel was injured."

The Warner sleigh was soon ready and Angel was let loose to lead the way. Mr. and Mrs. Ridley's fear was that their daughter would freeze to death before they found her. Or that she was dead already. "We didn't know what we would find when we reached her," said Mrs. Ridley.

Angel led them directly to Emily. She was still unconscious and half-frozen. Her parents bundled Emily in blankets and began the trip back to the farm.

When Emily regained consciousness that evening, her first words were, "Where's Angel?"

Unfortunately, Angel was lying in the barn half-dead herself. Her injury had been made worse by her run down the mountain and the return trip to find Emily.

"My father said Angel had to be put down," said Emily. "I knew Angel was in pain and I didn't want her to suffer. I had to say good-bye to Angel."

Angel will be buried near the Ridley barn.

"Angel was the best pony in the world," said Emily. "And she saved my life. I just wish I could have saved *her* life."

May Angel rest in peace. She is, indeed, an Angel.

Ghost Stories

A tear rolled down Anna's cheek. "That's such a sad story," she said.

"Angel was a wonderful pony," said Pam.

"Emily must have been *so* upset when her pony died," said Lulu.

"I bet that strange whinny we heard was Angel's ghost," Anna said. "And that horseshoe we found belonged to Angel."

Ms. McGee came back into her office. "What did you think of the article?" she asked.

"It was really sad," said Anna.

"We'd like to learn more about Ridley Farm," added Lulu. "Especially about Emily and her pony."

"You should talk to the Ridleys," said Ms. McGee. "Some of their great-grandchildren live in Wiggins."

"Who?" asked Anna.

"Well, there's Rick Conway," said Ms. McGee. "He's a great-grandson of Emily Ridley."

"Rick Conway who shoes horses?" asked Pam. "The farrier?"

"That's right," said Ms. McGee.

"I know him," said Pam. "He comes to our barn every month."

"Let's go back to my house and call him," said Anna.

Pam handed Ms. McGee the photo album, newspaper article, and gloves. "Can we come back another time and read more about Morristown?" she asked.

"I hope you will," said Ms. McGee. "We're

having a Wiggins Historical Fair to remember the early days in Wiggins and Morristown. Would you girls like to participate?"

The Pony Pals exchanged a glance and nodded. They all wanted to be part of the fair.

"We'd love to be in the fair," said Lulu.

"What do you want us to do?" asked Pam.

"I'll let you know in a couple of days," said Ms. McGee. "We're making plans for it now."

The Pony Pals thanked Ms. McGee. They ran across the town green to Anna's house, went into the kitchen, and gathered around the phone.

"You call Mr. Conway, Pam," said Anna. "He knows you."

"See if he'll let us interview him," said Lulu.

Pam looked up Mr. Conway's telephone number in the phone book and dialed the number. Lulu and Anna crossed their fingers for good luck.

Mr. Conway wasn't home, but Mrs. Conway spoke to Pam. When Pam hung up she told Anna and Lulu about the conversation. "Mrs. Conway said he's on his way to Olson's Horse Farm," Pam said. "If we want to talk to him we should go there."

"Let's go," said Anna.

The Pony Pals rode single file along Main Street and Belgo Road. When they came to the wide dirt trail that led to Olson's Horse Farm they went side by side.

"Let's ask Mr. Conway if he remembers any stories about Emily and Angel," said Lulu.

"And about ghosts in Morristown," added Anna.

Mr. Conway was in the barn putting horseshoes on Mr. Olson's thoroughbred horses.

"Hi, Mr. Conway," said Pam. "I'm Pam Crandal. You take care of the horses and ponies in my mother's riding school."

"Yup," said Mr. Conway without looking up. "I do."

"We heard that you're related to the Ridleys," said Lulu. "The ones who had a farm in Morristown."

"Yup," answered Mr. Conway.

The Pony Pals exchanged a glance. Mr. Conway was not going to be easy to interview.

"Did you ever hear any stories about your great-grandmother Emily Ridley?" asked Anna. "She lived on the farm about a hundred and fifty years ago."

"She died when I was a boy," mumbled Mr. Conway. He didn't look at the Pony Pals, but kept his eyes on his work.

"Do you remember anything about her?" asked Lulu.

"Did you hear any stories about when she was young?" asked Anna.

"Nope to the first question," said Mr. Conway. He banged a nail into a horse's foot. Anna jumped at the noise. "And nope to the second question," he added.

Finally, Mr. Conway looked at the Pony

Pals. "Why are you asking me all these questions?" he asked.

"Because we want to know about life in Morristown," said Pam.

"Before it was a ghost town," said Lulu.

"Well, it *is* a real ghost town," said Mr. Conway. "I'll say that for it."

"What do you mean?" asked Anna.

"The woods in those parts are haunted," said Mr. Conway.

"Do you think they're really haunted?" asked Lulu. "Or are those just stories."

"What happened to me is no story," said Mr. Conway. "It was real."

"Wh-wh-what happened to you?" stammered Anna.

"I used to ride up in those hills some," said Mr. Conway. "One day a storm comes on me. I'm riding in the rain, when right in front of me I see a pony. I figured it's a pony that got loose. I was going to tie it up behind my horse and bring it back to town." He lowered his voice and looked right into Anna's eyes. "But the pony vanished. Disappeared into thin air. Like magic. Or a ghost. I know four other people who saw that same ghost."

Anna gulped. Lulu took a deep breath. Pam rolled her eyes.

"Have you seen any other ghosts in Morristown?" asked Lulu.

"There's the crying-baby ghost," said Mr. Conway. "Heard that one. And the ghost of old Mr. Warner. He's a mean one. He's always rattling these chains and tripping people up on their walks in the woods. He cost me a sprained ankle once."

BANG! Mr. Conway hammered in another nail. This time all three girls jumped.

The Search

"I don't believe in ghosts," Pam told Mr. Conway. "Besides, we're more interested in the people who lived in Morristown than stories about ghosts."

Lulu took the horseshoe she dug up from Ridley Farm out of her backpack. "We found this," she said. She handed it to Mr. Conway. He studied it. "It looks like a pony's shoe," he said. He pointed to an engraved "R" at the top of the horseshoe. "That's our family mark. Where'd you say you found it?"

"We dug it up where the Ridley farmhouse used to be," said Lulu. "We've been finding a lot of interesting things there."

"What are you girls doing digging up the old farm?" asked Mr. Conway.

"We're interested in the past," answered Anna.

Mr. Conway shook his head. "I wouldn't be messing around with no past," he said.

"We just want to know more about how people lived back then," said Pam. "Especially your great-grandmother."

"We read a story about your great-grandmother," said Lulu. "How she was in an accident with her pony Angel. And how Angel saved her life."

"Heard that story myself," said Mr. Conway.

"Do you think this is Angel's shoe?" asked Lulu.

Mr. Conway handed the horseshoe back to Lulu. "Could be," he said.

"Can you tell us *anything* about Emily?" asked Lulu.

"Nope," said Mr. Conway. He picked up the horse's back right hoof and went back to work. The Pony Pals knew that the interview was over.

That night the Pony Pals had a barn sleepover at Pam's. Pam fell right to sleep. But Anna and Lulu were still awake.

"Lulu, do you really think there are ghosts in Morristown?" whispered Anna.

"Yes," said Lulu. "Mr. Conway really scared me."

"Are you afraid to go back there tomorrow?" asked Anna.

"A little," said Lulu. "I want to find out more about Ridley Farm."

"Me, too," said Anna.

"Let's look for Angel's grave," said Lulu.

Lulu and Anna stayed awake for a long time talking about the ghosts of Morristown — especially the ghost of Mr. Warner who tripped people with his chains. "I hope he doesn't trip our ponies," said Anna.

Lulu didn't answer. She had fallen asleep. Soon Anna was asleep, too.

The next morning the Pony Pals rode their ponies back to Morristown. Even Pam was a little afraid as they moved along the trails.

"I'd never come here at night," said Anna.

"Me, either," said Lulu.

"You're not supposed to ride in the woods at night anyway," said Pam.

When the Pony Pals reached Ridley Farm, they tied their ponies to the trees. They looked at the hole where Lulu had found the horseshoe.

"Why was a horseshoe in the house?" asked Lulu.

"Maybe Emily hung it on the wall," said Anna. "As a way to remember Angel."

"The newspaper article said that Angel was buried near the barn," said Lulu. "I wonder where the barn was."

Pam walked into a cluster of bushes. "I

saw a pile of stones in here the other day," she said. "Maybe the barn was here."

Lulu and Anna followed Pam into the bushes.

"I bet Emily made a marker for Angel's grave," said Anna.

"If we find the grave we could fix it up," said Lulu.

"Listen," whispered Pam. "I hear something."

The Pony Pals stood still. *Clop, clop. Clop, clop.* They all heard the sound of horses' hooves on the dirt trail. And a whinny.

Lightning nickered nervously.

"It's the ghost pony," whispered Anna in a shaky voice.

"*Whoa*," called a voice.

"With Mr. Warner's ghost," Anna added. "The one with the chains."

"I'm going to look," said Pam. "I'll prove it isn't a ghost."

"Don't!" whispered Lulu. "He'll see you."

"If it's a ghost, it knows we're here anyway," said Pam. She spread the bushes with her hands and stepped out.

Pam's heart pounded with fear. I have to stay calm, she told herself. I have to prove to Anna and Lulu that there are no such thing as ghosts.

A Visitor

Pam saw a man on a big gray horse. He was riding near the foundation of the Ridley farmhouse. She quickly hid behind a tree. "It's not a ghost," she whispered to Anna and Lulu in the bushes behind her. "It's a real man on a real horse."

Anna and Lulu came out from the bushes and stood next to Pam.

"It's Mr. Conway!" whispered Anna.

"What does he want?" asked Lulu.

"He probably wants to tell us more ghost

stories," whispered Pam. "I think he likes to scare us."

Just then Mr. Conway saw the Pony Pals. They waved and walked toward him.

"Hi, Mr. Conway," said Pam.

"We're surprised to see you," said Lulu.

"You girls got me to thinking about the old farm," Mr. Conway said in a gruff voice.

Anna patted the gray horse's nose.

"You have a nice horse," said Lulu.

"Thank you," said Mr. Conway. He looked around. "Haven't been here in years. I used to come up here with my mother."

"We were just trying to figure out where the barn was," said Pam. "Do you know?"

Mr. Conway looked to his right and left. He pointed to the bushes where Pam had found piles of stones. "I think it was over there," he said.

"We read that Angel's grave was near the barn," said Lulu.

"I remember pet graves in the back of the barn," said Mr. Conway. "There were a few slate grave markers there. Homemade ones.

Must have all been knocked down and grown over by now."

"We want to find Angel's grave and fix it right," said Anna.

"Is that okay?" asked Pam.

"Okay by me," said Mr. Conway. "It's a nice thing to do."

"Do you mind that we're digging up here?" Lulu asked Mr. Conway.

"Do you think we're bothering ghosts?" asked Anna.

"I don't mind," said Mr. Conway. "But I can't speak for the ghosts."

He turned his horse around and started to ride away.

Mr. Conway stopped his horse suddenly. "I almost forgot," he said. He motioned the Pony Pals to catch up with him.

"Probably another ghost story," mumbled Pam.

Mr. Conway looked down at them from his saddle. "I was telling my wife about you girls," he said. "And about all the snooping around that you've been doing. She's pretty interested in that history stuff, too."

"Does she know anything about the Ridleys?" asked Lulu.

"Not much," Mr. Conway answered. "But she thought she remembered seeing something belonging to Emily Ridley in our attic."

"What was it?" asked Anna.

"Was it from when Emily was young?" asked Lulu.

"Can we see it?" asked Pam.

They were all talking at once.

Mr. Conway put up a hand. "Now hold on," he said.

"Sorry," said the Pony Pals in unison.

"My wife went up to the attic. Took some searching, but she found a box of things that belonged to my great-grandmother Emily Ridley."

"What's in the box?" asked Lulu.

"Well, you'll have to ask Ms. McGee that," he said. "My wife said she'd take the box to the Historical Society. She's been helping with that historical fair they're going to have."

"Thanks," said Pam. "Thanks for telling us."

"Yup," said Mr. Conway. He turned his horse around and rode away.

"A box of Emily's things!" exclaimed Anna.

"Let's go see it right now," said Lulu.

"Don't get too excited," said Pam. "It might just be a sewing kit or something like that."

"I don't care," said Lulu. "Whatever it is, it will tell us something more about Emily."

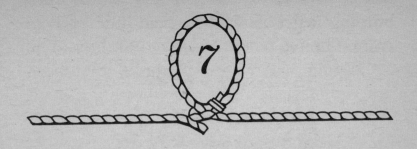

A Box of Treasures

An hour later the Pony Pals walked into the Wiggins Historical Society building. Ms. McGee looked up from her desk and smiled at the three girls. "I'm so glad you came over today," she said. "I have something to show you."

"Did Mrs. Conway bring you Emily's box?" asked Pam.

"Yes," said Ms. McGee. "That's what I wanted to show you." She handed each of the girls a pair of gloves. While they were putting them on, Ms. McGee reached into the bottom drawer of her desk and pulled out a small wooden box. She handed it to Lulu. The top of the box was hand-painted.

"Treasures!" exclaimed Anna.

"Can we look inside?" Pam asked Ms. McGee.

"Certainly," she answered.

The Pony Pals quickly sat themselves down on the couch. Pam opened the box.

The first thing Lulu noticed was a silver barrette. She held it in the palm of her hand.

"It's so pretty," said Anna.

"It looks handmade," said Pam. "I bet someone made it for Emily."

Anna took a bracelet out of the box. "A charm bracelet," she said. "Look what's on it."

"And look, a handkerchief," said Pam. She pulled a white lace-trimmed hanky from the box. "It has initials on it," said Lulu. "*E.R.* for Emily Ridley."

But Anna wasn't looking at the handkerchief. She was looking at something else in the box.

"Look!" she exclaimed. "Look at what was under the handkerchief."

Pam and Lulu looked. They saw a small

dark blue book with *My Diary* written in gold letters.

"Emily's diary!" exclaimed Anna.

Lulu reached into the box and lifted out the diary. It was tied closed with a yellow ribbon.

"Open it," said Anna.

"We can't read it," said Pam. "It's a diary. Diaries are private."

Ms. McGee looked up from her work at the desk. "Diaries from people who lived a long time ago tell us about their lives," she said. "It's okay for you to read Emily's diary. I did."

"You did?" said Anna.

"Emily reminds me a lot of you girls," said Ms. McGee.

"Did she love ponies?" asked Pam.

"Did she have friends to ride with like we do?" asked Anna.

Ms. McGee smiled at the Pony Pals. "You'll have to read the diary to find out," she said. "I have to make some phone calls now. Why don't you take the diary into the library where it's quiet. Bring the book back to me when you've finished reading it."

Lulu put the barrette, charm bracelet, and handkerchief back in the box. Pam closed the box and put it on Ms. McGee's desk. Anna held the diary close to her chest. The three girls went into the library and sat at the worktable in the middle of the room.

Emily's diary! They couldn't wait to read what Emily had written.

The Diary

October 2, 1869
Dearest Diary,

You are my wonderful birthday present from my mother and father. I have never written in a diary and do not know what I should write. I guess I will start by telling you about myself.

I am ten years old and live on a farm in Morristown. I have two older brothers, a sister who is one year younger than me, and a baby brother who is only four years old. My mother was a schoolteacher before she married my father. She is always making us practice our reading, writing, and arithmetic at home. My two best friends are Lucy Chatfield and my sister Meg. Actually, the three of us are best friends.

Lucy lives on the farm next to ours. We three play together whenever we can. Sometimes we help one another with chores. Yesterday, Meg and I helped Lucy pick apples from her orchard. Today, before my birthday dinner, Lucy, Meg, and I made bread.

Meg and Lucy are my best friends, but my dearest friend is an animal. Her name is Angel and she is my pony. I have had Angel since I was five. Angel wants to be with me all of the time. And I want to be with her.

My sister, Meg, has her own pony. His name is Dapple. Dapple has white spots all over his gray coat. Dapple and Angel are both very strong and pull the plow for Father. But even after Dapple and Angel work hard all day, they still love to go riding with us in the woods. We like the trail between our fields and Lucy's fields best.

Lucy has a pony, too. Lucy's pony's name is Candy. Her name suits her because she is a very sweet pony.

We are three girls and three ponies. We have the most wonderful times together.

That's all for now, dear diary. I will write in you every day. I promise.

November 4, 1869
Dearest Diary,

I did not keep my promise to write in you every day. I have been very busy with chores and schoolwork. Lucy, Meg, and I all go to school together. The school is a long way from our farms. Sometimes we ride our ponies to school, but mostly we walk.

There are twenty students in our school. The youngest student is my brother Ethan. He is four years old. The oldest student is seventeen. Our teacher is Mrs. Wright. She is very strict, but I think she has a kind heart. There are times when the older boys pester the younger girls, especially Lucy, Meg, and me. I mostly like school. Except in the morning before the wood stove heats the room.

Today I did not ride Angel to school. And guess what she did? My smart pony unhitched the gate with her teeth and came to school on her own. I was doing my sums, when I heard some of the other children laughing. I looked up and saw Angel looking through the window at me. I burst out laughing, too. Even Mrs. Wright had a smile on her face. Then she became stern again and said that I had to bring Angel home and come back to school.

I have to say good-bye for now, dear diary. It is time to do my homework in long division. Also I am very tired from all that walking.

January 1, 1870
Dearest Diary,
This is the first day of the year 1870. My resolutions for the new year are:
1. Be kind to all persons, even those who pester me.
2. Do my chores without being asked.
3. Be nice to my brothers and sister.
4. Waste nothing and save even the smallest piece of string.

5. Write in my diary at least once a week.

January 10, 1870
Dearest Diary,
   Yesterday was the saddest day of my life. My dear pony Angel died. She died because she saved my life. We will bury Angel near the barn.
   I am too sad to write anymore.

January 12, 1870
Dearest Diary,
   Today we buried Angel's body on the south side of the barn. I put a slate marker on her grave. I wrote a poem about Angel and painted her picture in black paint on the slate. This is what it looks like:

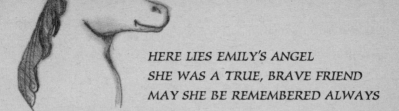

HERE LIES EMILY'S ANGEL
SHE WAS A TRUE, BRAVE FRIEND
MAY SHE BE REMEMBERED ALWAYS

My whole family and Lucy stood by the graveside with me. As we buried Angel I remembered the first time I saw her. It was Christmas morning. We were finishing up a special Christmas breakfast. Suddenly, we heard the jingle of bells outside. "I wonder what that is?" said my mother. "Let's go see."

The whole family got up from the table. We grabbed our coats and hurried outside. There, in front of the house, was a pony pulling a sleigh. The pony's harness was covered with bells and red ribbons.

"Merry Christmas, Emily!" shouted my brothers and sister. Angel looked at us and shook her head. The bells rang louder than ever and we all laughed. My father lifted me in his arms and we went over to Angel. I gave her a kiss on her forehead and put my arms around her neck. She was my very own pony. I will miss her forever.

Clues From Emily

Lulu flipped through the rest of the diary. "That's the last thing she wrote in this diary," she said.

"I feel like I know Emily now," Anna said.

"Emily, Meg, and Lucy," Pam said. "They were three friends with ponies, just like us."

The girls went back to Ms. McGee's office. Anna handed her Emily's diary. "I'm glad that we could find out more about Emily," she said.

"She loved her pony a lot," said Lulu. "Just like us."

"Come back and look at the diary any time," said Ms. McGee. "Now I'd like to ask you girls to do me a favor."

"What?" asked the Pony Pals together.

"Remember, I told you about the Wiggins Historical Fair?" she said. "Well, we wondered if you girls would dress in the kind of clothes Emily and her friends wore. We have the costumes."

The Pony Pals looked at one another and smiled. They all wanted to do it.

"Can our ponies be in the fair, too?" asked Anna.

"Absolutely," said Ms. McGee. "Ponies were an important part of life back then."

"Acorn is a driving pony," said Anna. "I can give kids rides in his cart."

"Cart rides would be a wonderful addition to the fair," said Ms. McGee.

"And we can give regular pony rides on our ponies," said Lulu.

"Lightning and Snow White love to do that," added Pam.

"And why don't you make a display of the items you found on Ridley Farm," said Ms. McGee.

"Sure," said Lulu.

"Maybe you'll write about life back then," said Ms. McGee.

"We can do that, too," said Pam.

The girls said good-bye to Ms. McGee and headed across the town green toward Anna's house.

"I think it'll be great fun to be in the fair and make posters about Ridley Farm," said Pam.

"But what about Angel's grave?" asked Lulu. "Did you forget about that?"

"I think we should look for it first thing tomorrow," said Anna.

"I thought you were afraid of ghosts," said Pam.

"I'm not afraid of Angel's ghost," said Anna.

"Me, neither," said Lulu.

"Emily would want us to find Angel's grave and fix it up," said Anna.

"*If* we can find it," said Pam. "And that's a big *if*."

"We have to try," said Lulu.

The next morning the Pony Pals rode out to Ridley Farm.

They dismounted and took off their ponies' bridles.

Pam stroked Lightning's neck. She was thinking about how awful she'd feel if something happened to Lightning. Pam looked over at Anna and Lulu stroking their ponies. She knew they felt the same way.

"Let's keep our ponies near us today," suggested Pam.

"Maybe they'll help us find Angel's grave," added Anna.

"Now, let's make a plan for finding the grave," said Pam. She sat on the stone wall. Lulu and Anna sat beside her. Their ponies grazed next to them.

"Emily gave us a clue in her diary for finding the grave," said Pam. "She wrote, *We buried Angel on the south side of the barn.*"

Lulu pointed in front of them. "South is that direction."

Pam jumped off the stone wall. "And Mr. Conway said that he thought the barn was over there," she said. "Where I found those stones."

"There was another clue in the diary," said Lulu. "Emily said that the gravestone was a piece of slate. But it's probably all broken by now. So we should look for pieces of slate."

"And Emily wrote on the slate in black paint," said Anna. "A piece of slate with black letters would be a big clue."

"They could be very small pieces of slate," said Pam. "And there are a lot of bushes and tall grass to go through."

"Then we should get started," said Anna.

Two hours later the Pony Pals were still looking through the bushes and grass for

69

Angel's gravesite. They'd found a lot of stones, but no slate.

"Let's take a break and walk our ponies," suggested Lulu.

The girls untied their ponies and led them to a grassy spot. Acorn pulled on his lead rope. He wanted to go into a bushy area. Anna let go of the lead rope and he pushed his way into the bushes. He lowered his head and sniffed the ground.

"Acorn," said Pam with a laugh. "What are you doing?"

"I think he's looking for something," whispered Anna.

Acorn took a few more steps and sniffed the ground again. Finally, he stopped and pawed the ground. Anna bent over. "Give me the shovel," she told Lulu. "Hold Acorn," she told Pam.

Anna dug into the ground exactly where Acorn had pawed. Her shovel hit something hard. She cleared away dirt and pulled a piece of slate from the ground. "Look what Acorn found!" exclaimed Anna.

Puzzling Clues

Lulu bent down to see what Acorn had found.

"There are letters on it," said Anna excitedly.

"And they're in black paint," added Pam.

"I guess it wasn't Angel's grave marker," said Lulu.

"The Ridleys must have had a pet named *Ed*," said Lulu.

Anna patted Acorn's side. "Good try, Acorn. But it's not Angel's grave."

Pam studied the piece of slate that Acorn and Anna found. "Wait a minute," she said. "I think this is part of Angel's gravestone. Remember what Emily wrote on the grave?"

"Here lies Emily's Angel," began Anna.

"She was a true, brave friend," continued Lulu.

"May she be remembered always," said Pam. "E-D is the end of the word *remembered*. So *ED ALWAYS* is the end of the last line."

"I bet you're right, Pam," said Anna.

"Let's look for more pieces of slate around here," said Lulu. "Maybe we'll find more words."

"It's like pieces of a jigsaw puzzle," said Pam.

The Pony Pals dropped to their hands

and knees and raked the grass with their tools.

"I found another piece of slate," shouted Lulu. "It says *HERE LIES.*"

"And here's one that says, *BRAVE FR,*" said Pam.

"I found the last part of the word *FRIEND*," said Lulu. She held up a piece of slate with *IEND* printed on it.

Anna put her arms around Acorn's neck and gave him a hug. "Thank you, Acorn," she said. "Thank you for finding Angel's grave."

"Let's clean up around it," said Lulu.

The girls pulled weeds and raked the area around the grave. When they finished that job, they rode their ponies back to Pam's. It was time to make a new marker for Angel's grave.

Pam found a piece of slate in the garage. Her mother said they could have it and told them where to find black paint and brushes.

The girls brought the slate and their

supplies out to the big, flat rock near the paddock. Anna painted a running pony at the top of the slate. Next, Pam and Lulu wrote Emily's words under the painting.

"How are we going to get this big piece of slate to the Ridley Farm?" asked Pam. "A car can't drive on those trails."

"But a pony cart can," said Anna. "We can put the slate in Acorn's cart. He can take Angel's new grave marker to Ridley Farm."

"It'll be just like in olden times when they didn't have cars," said Lulu.

"Now we should work on our display for the Wiggins Historical Fair," said Pam.

The Pony Pals spent the rest of the day at the Historical Society. They learned more about life in Morristown, a hundred and fifty years before they were born.

When the girls finished their project for the fair, Ms. McGee brought out old-fashioned dresses for them to try on. The dresses were long and very full. The three girls looked at themselves in the mirror.

"Emily had to wear a dress like this every day," said Pam.

"Even when she rode her pony," added Anna.

"I'm glad girls wear jeans and leggings now," said Lulu.

Anna turned around so that her skirt swished around her. "It's fun to wear a long dress," said Anna. "I can't wait for the fair."

Anna didn't have to wait long. The Old Time Fair was the next day. Pam rode over to Anna's and Lulu's early in the morning. The girls groomed their ponies and then put on their costumes. After saddling up Snow White and Lightning and hitching Acorn to his cart, the Pony Pals were ready for the fair on the town green.

The town green was filled with stands and booths for food, games, and exhibits. Anna's father was doing a woodworking demonstration on how to join pieces of wood without using nails. Pam's neighbors, the Olsons, had a stand. Mr. Olson was showing how you shear a sheep. And Mrs. Olson was spinning wool. "There's the Off-Main Diner booth," said Pam. She was pointing to a big tent in the middle of the green.

"My mom is making ice cream with an old-style ice-cream-making machine," said Anna.

"Look at those kids," said Lulu. Pam and Anna saw four children rolling big hoops along the path that cut through the green.

Everything in the center of Wiggins was the way it was in olden times. Best of all, no cars were allowed on Main Street or Upper Main Street.

The Pony Pals walked their ponies across the town green toward the Historical Society building. A crowd of kids followed them.

"I want the first ride in Acorn's cart," said Rosalie Lacey. Anna and Lulu exchanged a smile. The Pony Pals liked Rosalie Lacey.

"I rode Lightning last time," said a little

boy with curly black hair. "Today, I'm going to ride Snow White."

"Lightning is my favorite pony," said a girl. "Her hair is the same color as mine. I want to ride her."

A riding ring was set up for the ponies in front of the Historical Society. It was a perfect spot for pony rides on Lightning and Snow White.

Anna drove Acorn over to the library. A line of children were waiting there for a cart ride around the town green. Rosalie Lacey climbed into Acorn's cart and sat next to Anna.

"I like your dress," Rosalie told Anna. "You look pretty."

"Thank you," said Anna.

"I went to the movies last night," said Rosalie.

"I don't know about movies," said Anna. "I live in 1860. Movies haven't been invented yet."

"Really?" exclaimed Rosalie.

"We don't have television, electric lights,

running water, or airplanes. We don't even have cars. You need your pony to take you places. The only other way to travel is by foot."

"Wow!" said Rosalie.

Lulu and Pam also told the children who took pony rides about life in the 1870's.

After the pony and cart rides, the children went into the Historical Society to see the Pony Pals' display, *A VISIT TO THE PAST*.

A VISIT TO THE PAST

by Pam Crandal, Anna Harley, and Lulu Sanders

We like to ride our ponies on the trails near Mt. Morris. There used to be many farms in that area. We wanted to learn more about life on those farms a hundred and fifty years ago. We learned about a girl named Emily Ridley.

Emily was ten years old in 1870. Her best friends were her sister, Meg, and their friend, Lucy. These three girls loved ponies, just like we do.

Daily life on a farm in Morristown was hard work for girls and boys. They had adult responsibilities and spent many hours a day helping with farm and house chores.

Emily's chores included:

- tending the fire
- cooking, baking, and cleaning in the kitchen
- making butter and cheese
- taking care of her younger brother
- spinning yarn
- darning clothing
- feeding the animals
- helping with planting, weeding, and harvesting

Emily's life was very busy. But she was still full of fun.

HOW EMILY, MEG, AND LUCY DRESSED

For every day, girls wore a dress that was loose and went to their ankles. They wore a long apron or pinafore over the dress. The apron was to keep their dresses clean. Most farm girls only had one or two every-day dresses. They never wore pants.

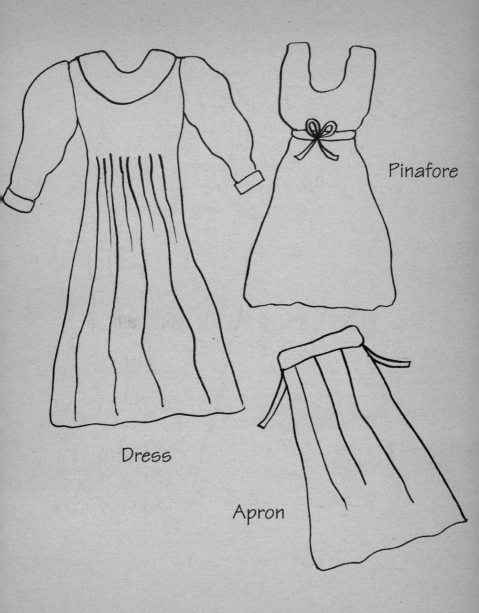

Pinafore

Dress

Apron

Girls wore a cotton dress under their clothes. This dress was called a shift.

At night, the girls wore the shift to bed. It was easy to get ready for bed in the 1870's.

Girls wore cotton or wool stockings.

Shift

Each of the girls had a best dress she
saved for Sundays and holidays.

This is the kind of hat Emily and her friends might have worn. It would be pinned to the top of their hair. Most girls kept their hair long.

If Emily, Meg, and Lucy were young girls today, they would be our Pony Pals.

Good-bye, Angel

When the fair ended, the girls met Ms. McGee in front of the Historical Society. "Thank you, girls," she said. "The fair was a great success. You three did a terrific job." She patted Snow White on the head. "So did your ponies."

"It was fun," said Anna.

Lightning rubbed her cheek on Pam's shoulder. "Our ponies had a good time, too," said Pam.

"Can we bring back the clothes tomorrow?" asked Lulu. "We want to wear them a little longer."

"Certainly," said Ms. McGee.

The Pony Pals thanked Ms. McGee and went back to Anna's house. Lulu and Anna put riding pants on under their dresses. Then the three girls put Angel's new gravestone in Acorn's cart. It was time to ride out to Ridley Farm.

Anna and Acorn took the lead onto Main Street. Lulu and Pam followed on their ponies.

When they reached the farm, they rode up to the grave site. Pam and Lulu dug around the broken base of the old grave marker. Pam pulled the broken pieces out. Lulu and Anna lifted the slate out of the cart and placed it upright in the ground. Pam packed the dirt around the base of the new grave marker so the slate wouldn't tip over.

The Pony Pals and their ponies stood in a circle around the new grave marker. The girls were all thinking about Emily and her

Pony Pals, Meg and Lucy. It felt like there were six Pony Pals standing around Angel's grave.

"We're doing this for Angel," whispered Anna.

"And Emily," said Lulu.

"Let's say the poem now," said Pam.

The Pony Pals recited:

"Here lies Emily's Angel.

Angel was a true, brave friend.

May she be remembered always."

"May Angel rest in peace," said Pam.

"Good-bye, Angel," said Anna and Lulu together.

Snow White nickered softly. Acorn nuzzled against Anna's shoulder. And Lightning nodded her head.

The girls walked their ponies back toward the trail. They would always remember Angel, the ghost pony.

Dear Reader:

I am having a lot of fun researching and writing books about the Pony Pals. I've met many interesting kids and adults who love ponies. And I've visited some wonderful ponies at homes, farms, and riding schools.

Before writing Pony Pals I wrote fourteen novels for children and young adults. Four of these were honored by Children's Choice Awards.

I live in Sharon, Connecticut, with my husband, Lee, and our dog, Willie. Our daughter is all grown up and has her own apartment in New York City.

Besides writing novels I like to draw, paint, garden, and swim. I didn't have a pony when I was growing up, but I have always loved them and dreamt about riding. Now I take riding lessons on a horse named Saz.

I like reading and writing about ponies as much as I do riding. Which proves to me that you don't have to ride a pony to love them. And you certainly don't need a pony to be a Pony Pal.

Happy Reading,

Jeanne Betancourt

Get to know
AMBER BROWN
by Paula Danziger

She's funny, spunky, and unforgettable! Catch up on the hilarious and heartwarming adventures of Amber Brown as she loses a friend, travels to Europe, and starts a new school year.

☐ BBR45899-X	Amber Brown Is Not a Crayon	$2.99
☐ BBR50207-7	You Can't Eat Your Chicken Pox, Amber Brown	$2.99
☐ BBR93425-2	Amber Brown Goes Fourth	$2.99
☐ BBR94716-8	Amber Brown Wants Extra Credit	$3.50

The Adventures of THE BAILEY SCHOOL KIDS ®

Creepy, weird, wacky and funny things happen to the Bailey School Kids!™ Collect and read them all!

Available wherever you buy books, or use this order form

Scholastic Inc., P.O. Box 7502, Jefferson City, MO 65102

Please send me the books I have checked above. I am enclosing $_____ (please add $2.00 to cover shipping and handling). Send check or money order — no cash or C.O.D.s please.

Name _____

Address _____

City_____ State/Zip_____

Please allow four to six weeks for delivery. Offer good in the U.S. only. Sorry, mail orders are not available to residents of Canada. Prices subject to change.   BSK397

THE Berenstain BEAR® SCOUTS

by Stan & Jan Berenstai~~n~~

☐ BBF60384-1	The Berenstain Bear Scouts and the Coughing Catfish	$2.9
☐ BBF60380-9	The Berenstain Bear Scouts and the Humongous Pumpkin	$2.9
☐ BBF60385-X	The Berenstain Bear Scouts and the Sci-Fi Pizza	$2.9
☐ BBF94473-8	The Berenstain Bear Scouts and the Sinister Smoke Ring	$3.5
☐ BBF60383-3	The Berenstain Bear Scouts and the Terrible Talking Termite	$2.9
☐ BBF60386-8	The Berenstain Bear Scouts Ghost Versus Ghost	$2.9
☐ BBF60379-5	The Berenstain Bear Scouts in Giant Bat Cave	$2.9
☐ BBF60381-7	The Berenstain Bear Scouts Meet Bigpaw	$2.9
☐ BBF60382-5	The Berenstain Bear Scouts Save That Backscratcher	$2.9
☐ BBF94475-4	The Berenstain Bear Scouts and the Magic Crystal Caper	$3.5
☐ BBF94477-0	The Berenstain Bear Scouts and the Run-Amuck Robot	$3.5
☐ BBF94479-7	The Berenstain Bear Scouts and the Ice Monster	$3.5

© 1995 Berenstain Enterprises, Inc.
Available wherever you buy books or use this order form.

- -

Send orders to:
Scholastic Inc., P.O. Box 7502, 2931 East McCarty Street, Jefferson City, MO 65102-7502

Please send me the books I have checked above. I am enclosing $_____ (please
add $2.00 to cover shipping and handling). Send check or money order — no cash o~~r~~
C.O.D.s please.

Name_____ Birthdate____/____/__

Address_____ M   D   Y

City_____ State_____ Zip_____

Please allow four to six weeks for delivery. Offer good in U.S.A. only. Sorry, mail orders are not available to residents of Canada.
Prices subject to change.

BB5